THE MAGICAL UNICORN SOCIETY
THE
DARK HEART
UNICORNS

Michael O'Mara Books Limited

With special thanks to Melanie Reynard

Edited by Emma Taylor
Designed by Claire Cater and Jack Clucas
Cover design by Angie Allison

Cover illustration by Jazlyn Alcaide
Interior illustrations by Jazlyn Alcaide, Chris Coady,
Mariano Epelbaum and Jose R Ibáñez

First published in Great Britain in 2024 by Michael O'Mara Books
Limited, 9 Lion Yard, Tremadoc Road, London SW4 7NQ

W www.mombooks.com
f Michael O'Mara Books
𝕏 @OMaraBooks
@omarabooks

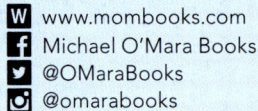

A CIP catalogue record for this book is available from the British Library.

ISBN: 978-1-78929-667-9

2 4 6 8 10 9 7 5 3 1

Printed in China

THE MAGICAL UNICORN SOCIETY
THE
DARK HEART
UNICORNS

Compiled by
Indira Jenkins

CONTENTS

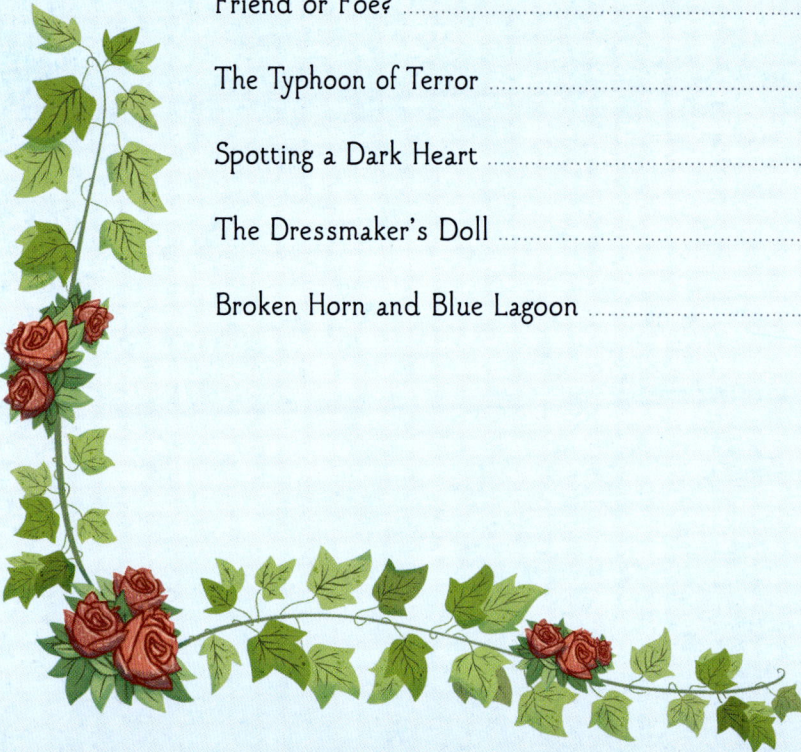

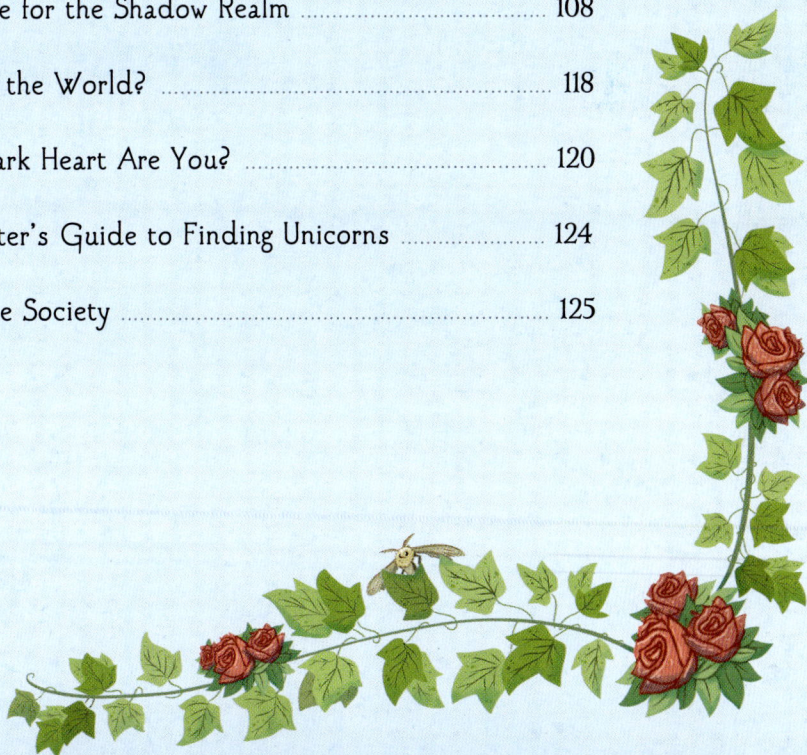

WELCOME

My name is Indira Jenkins and I suppose I'm like lots of people. I like to read books, create art and listen to music. However, I have a secret. I'm part of the Magical Unicorn Society, or the MUS as it is known to its members. I'm not the youngest member of the MUS by far, but at thirteen I am one of the youngest adventurers.

Most of my family are in the MUS and, even though sightings are rare, they've all been lucky enough to see a unicorn. My parents have dedicated their lives to the study of these elusive, mystical creatures, and growing up seeing their work made me hopeful that I would one day see a unicorn, too.

Not long after my twelfth birthday, my wish came true and I finally got to see not one, but three unicorns. My Great Uncle Selwyn is the President of the society and last summer he invited my family on an exciting research expedition. It was on this trip that I finally got to see the unicorns, including a very special and rare unicorn indeed.

Up until now, the MUS has recorded eight unicorn families, or 'blessings' as they are known. However, while on Uncle Selwyn's expedition, an astonishing archaeological discovery confirmed evidence of a ninth, previously undocumented blessing, called Dark Hearts. This unicorn family has always existed, although their true nature and story have been kept hidden for hundreds of years.

It seems that both humans and the other unicorn families have misunderstood Dark Hearts. Some accounts present them as a force of evil, sent from a dark parallel realm to cause chaos and destruction in our world. As unicorns are celebrated around the world for their magic and as a force for good, it is not surprising that the existence of Dark Hearts has been concealed. In fact, dark magic caused the creation of all the unicorns. Legend says that centuries ago, two ordinary horses became the first ever unicorns as an evil Winter Dragon chased them through a magical waterfall. They became known as the Golden and Silver Unicorns.

Now, new evidence has come to light, and what is clear is that the Dark Hearts are far from evil. The first part of this evidence was found in a Himalayan temple, pieced together from stone tablets and untranslated scriptures. I'm delighted to share its findings with you in this book.

The pages that follow detail some of the extraordinary encounters of ordinary people, as well as fearless explorers, with this new blessing of unicorns. I hope you enjoy reading these exciting tales, and that one day you're lucky enough to see a unicorn for yourself.

Indira Jenkins

From cities to hilltops and swirling seas,

A unicorn's magic runs wild and free.

THE UNICORN FAMILIES

There are eight other unicorn families that appear in this book.
Find out their magical abilities and unique appearances below.

WATER MOONS

Water Moons love being near water.
They're known for helping sailors and
fishermen when they're in need.

SHADOW NIGHTS

These unicorns often appear in
dreams or at times of great distress.
Their coats are flecked with stars.

WOODLAND FLOWERS

Wild flowers fill these unicorns' manes
and tails. They are known for their affinity
for nature and special healing magic.

ICE WANDERERS

Ice Wanderer's horns are made of ice
or pearl. They live in cold climates and
can communicate across vast distances.

STORM CHASERS

These unicorns can control the elements, such as thunder and lightning. Their manes and tails crackle with electricity.

MOUNTAIN JEWELS

Mountain Jewels are the strongest of all the unicorn families. Their horns are made of opal or coral.

DESERT FLAMES

Known for being some of the fastest unicorns of all, they also have the power of flight.

DAWN SPIRITS

These unicorns only appear early in the morning and their manes shimmer with the colours of the dawn.

The Golden Unicorn and the Silver Unicorn also feature in this book. They were the first ever unicorns in existence, and the most powerful of them all.

The Dark Hearts

The MUS is still gathering information but, as we uncover more historical evidence, it appears that the rather unusual and elusive Dark Hearts have been around for a very long time, right under our noses. Most of the reported sightings have been misinterpreted or kept secret — until now. Here's what we know so far.

HOW MANY DARK HEARTS ARE THERE?

There have been reported sightings of eight different Dark Hearts. However, this number could be far greater, and now that we've shared our findings, we expect more to be discovered over the coming months and years.

Blue Lagoon

DO THEY HAVE ANY SPECIAL QUALITIES?

All the unicorn blessings have their own unique characteristics, and Dark Hearts are no exception. They have strong telepathic abilities, which enable them to communicate with each other and with humans. They can adopt the powers of other blessings while in their presence and therefore they can fly, gallop at great speeds and are impressively strong. Most striking of all, Dark Hearts are able to absorb and diffuse dark magic, rendering it harmless.

WHO LEADS THEM?

The Dark Hearts have two leaders, a male unicorn called Broken Horn and a female unicorn called Blue Lagoon.

Broken Horn

The Day
of the Eclipse

*Translated by members of the MUS from newly
discovered scriptures and stone tablets.*

As the age of unicorns began to thrive, so it was
that the evil Winter Dragons were purged
from our world. But evil is hard to vanquish
completely and often finds a way to persist.

The last Winter Dragon lay dying, defeated by the Golden and Silver Unicorns. Its final act was to strike out at a human man, scratching him with its poisonous claw. The poison coursed through the man's veins, turning him into an indestructible Demon King. For a time, he brought darkness and destruction to our world, but the unicorns used the magic of their horns to banish him to a realm of shadows where he could do no harm.

However, by allowing him to live a shadow of a life, his wicked heart burned with revenge. For centuries, he plotted to bring about the end of the unicorns with his evil magic. So powerful, his magic could often be felt on Earth in the form of violent storms and tremors.

Using the power of an eclipse, he caused an earthquake that split apart the mountains and created a tear between worlds. Out of the void he sent a huge, terrible five-headed dragon to destroy life in our world. One head spat fire, another venom and a third shot lightning bolts from its gigantic jaws. The other two heads had vicious teeth to snap up any animals or humans that were unlucky enough to become its prey. The scaly body of the dragon was so immense and the people of the mountains prayed for a miracle to save them.

The Golden and Silver Unicorns heard people crying for help and came to battle the dragon. It screamed and snapped as they pushed it back into the cave from where it had come.

However, the eclipse did not end. It would only end if the dragon was slain. All life on Earth was at risk, so the Golden and Silver Unicorns summoned the other blessings to join in the fight.

Storm Chasers manipulated the weather, sending clouds that crackled with electricity to strike the creature, while Woodland Flowers used their healing powers to cure the animals and humans that had been poisoned by the dragon. Water Moons directed jets of river water at the fire-breathing head and Dawn Spirits attacked it from the skies. But even with all of their special unicorn powers combined, it was not enough to defeat the dragon.

Harnessing the energy of the eclipsed Sun, the Silver Unicorn touched its horn to the ground to create a new blessing of unicorns that could help defend the world. Emerging from the shadows with pure hearts, the Dark Hearts were born.

As they appeared, the dragon burst out of the cave and hurled a bolt of lightning. The brunt of the strange, supernatural energy surged into the Silver Unicorn's horn and, although it was unharmed, the crackling energy rebounded on to the new family of unicorns. The magic fizzled into the ground and it appeared that the Silver Unicorn and Dark Hearts were unaffected.

The wind howled and thunder boomed in the dark skies as the new unicorns began to explore their environment. But unlike the other unicorn families, who had been born in a world that was peaceful and calm, with sunny skies and twinkling stars, it soon became apparent that Dark Hearts were very different to their cousins, not only in their appearance, but also in their magical abilities.

The Dark Hearts had black coats and onyx horns. Their many-coloured manes and tails swished from side to side with a curious, volatile energy. The Silver Unicorn tried to guide its new offspring, but they bucked and kicked, unable to keep still with their wild and unpredictable natures.

The Golden and Silver Unicorns quickly realized that the Dark Hearts didn't have full control of their powers yet, so they commanded the other blessings to rally together for another joint assault. At first, the Dark Hearts watched, but when they saw the other unicorn families moving into a formation, they cantered alongside them and tried to imitate their movements.

To help corner the beastly five-headed dragon, some Dark Hearts attempted to walk on the surface of a stream like Water Moons, but they failed, sending water and silt flying into the air.

Another group of Dark Hearts tried to mimic Storm Chasers, who were driving up a twister of dust to confuse the dragon. But instead of helping, their uncontrollable energy dispersed the tornado and allowed the dragon to send a bolt of lightning into the forest, setting it ablaze. Fortunately, three Ice Wanderers were able to quickly tackle the flames with an icy blast of magic from their horns. With disaster averted, they turned on the Dark Hearts and gave them cold and disapproving stares.

The Dark Hearts were desperately struggling to work out exactly what their powers were and how to control them. Their presence only seemed to create more chaos and embolden the dragon.

As the other unicorns battled to push the dragon back into the chasm, some of the younger Dark Hearts seemed completely oblivious to the jeopardy they were all in. Instead, their curiosity made them wander off to explore. Not before long, a group of them foolishly collided with a band of Desert Flames that were trying to set a trap for the dragon. This was the last straw and they finally lost the goodwill and support of the other blessings.

The largest of the Dark Hearts, a male with a tawny coloured mane and tail, had been watching closely from a distance. He knew that his family had not meant to cause trouble and he wanted to win back the support of the other blessings.

Away from the forest, he could see a group of Mountain Jewels working as a team and was eager to join them. They were galloping over the mountainside, driving the menacing beast backwards into the cave.

As the Dark Heart unicorn bravely leapt forward to offer his help, the Golden Unicorn raced past him. It was leading the pack of Mountain Jewels into a battle formation and commanding them to use all of their magic to slay the five-headed dragon once and for all. Using every bit of his strength, the Dark Heart unicorn tried to imitate them, but his hooves battered the mountainside so hard that it created a landslide.

A shard of rock flew through the air and hit his horn, chipping off the tip and leaving a jagged edge. His anguished whinny was so loud and piercing that it caused even more of the rock face to shatter and crash downwards towards the village.

The noise from the landslide was almost deafening and it caused all of the unicorns to career off in different directions, away from the dragon. The Mountain Jewels and the Golden Unicorn reared backwards, narrowly avoiding being crushed by the falling rocks.

In the chaos, the dragon seized the chance to break out of the cave. The Silver Unicorn desperately tried to round up the Dark Hearts in order to keep them under control, while the Golden Unicorn brought all of the other blessings together. One last time, they would try to push the dragon back into the dark, mysterious void from which it had sprung.

The unicorns assembled into a semi-circle around the beast. They pointed their glimmering horns at the dragon, directing a dazzling beam of pure energy at its leathery hide. It screamed as though the light was burning its scaly body and, even though the unicorn magic seemed to be working, still the beast held firm. Their power alone was not enough and they needed the Dark Hearts to help. If they all stood together, it might tip the balance in their favour.

The Dark Heart with the broken horn knew that this might be the last chance for his family to regain their honour. He was determined to master his magical skills and help defeat the dragon. Seeing that the Silver Unicorn had finally decided to abandon rounding up his brothers and sisters, he took the task upon himself and encouraged the unruly bunch to copy their more dignified cousins.

Leading the Dark Hearts into the fight, Broken Horn pointed his onyx stump at the dragon. The other Dark Hearts followed suit and bowed their heads with purpose.

Instead of sending out a glowing beam of magic like the other blessings had done, a mysterious mist shimmered over the Dark Hearts' coats and manes. The dragon roared in pain and dark magic surged out of its body, crackling through the Dark Hearts from horn to hoof and then into the ground. It was as if they had sucked the life out of the beast. The five dragon heads writhed and flopped. It was weakening.

Broken Horn reared up on to his hind legs. Suddenly, some of the strange energy surged back through his horn like a lightning rod and he sent a flash of light into the mountainside. The mountain trembled and an earthquake caused a shelf of rock to crash down on top of the writhing monster.

The dragon was finally crushed and its heads became lifeless. However, the rubble kept falling and tumbled down towards the forest at the base of the mountains. It was a catastrophe and it threatened to destroy everything in sight. The Golden and Silver Unicorns were quick to react and used their magical powers to create a force field.

The glowing shield protected all of the unicorns and repelled the rock, stopping it from obliterating the forest and villagers. A disaster had been averted, but only just.

With the five-headed dragon gone, the eclipse came to an end and, as the dust settled, the radiant Sun cast light on to the forest once again. Birds broke into song and the villagers cheered in relief.

The Golden Unicorn tossed its mane and snorted at the Dark Hearts in disapproval. Broken Horn bowed his head in shame. Even though the Dark Hearts had helped to defeat the dragon, their magic was just too wild and erratic. After all, the earthquake had nearly destroyed everything. The Dark Heart unicorns meant well, but unless they found a way to harness their strange powers, they were likely to cause more harm.

It is unclear whether the Golden Unicorn sent them, or if the Dark Hearts decided to go willingly, but Broken Horn led his brothers and sisters into the chasm — straight into the Shadow Realm.

With the dragon vanquished at last, the tear between our world and the Shadow Realm healed itself. However, the Dark Hearts were trapped forever in the Shadow Realm. Their sacrifice meant that the Demon King and his evil monsters could be kept from Earth and peace would return.

The Shadow Realm

This parallel world is a dark and inhospitable place filled with desolate mountains and valleys. The climate is dry and food is scarce. With the help of their magic, the Dark Hearts have learnt to adapt to this environment, but its harsh conditions have taken a toll and they long to return to the human world.

THE DARK HEARTS' HOME

When they were banished, the Dark Hearts searched for
a safe place to call their home. They found a dried-up
riverbed, surrounded by a forest of blackened trees.
A Dark Heart unicorn used its magic to keep
a warm fire burning during the cold nights.

SOURCES OF FOOD

There is little vegetation, so the Shadow Realm's
creatures have to scavenge and fight over whatever they
can find. However, a Dark Heart unicorn is able to use its
special powers to help make plants grow. The unicorns
can also use their magic to extract minerals from the
rocks and soil in order to help them survive.

THE DEMON KING'S DOMAIN

All of the evil creatures inside the Shadow Realm
are controlled by the Demon King. Under his orders,
the trolls created a throne for him, which they
carved out of rock into the side of a mountain.

The Shadow Realm
and the Demon King

*Written by Indira Jenkins
using field trip research.*

I'm sure you're wondering what the
Shadow Realm is like and I can
tell you. How do I know? Well, I've been
there, but that's a story for another time
and we have to start at the beginning
when the Dark Hearts first arrived.

Before the Demon King ravaged the land, the Shadow Realm was a beautiful place, filled with rainbows, magnificent trees, waterfalls and magical creatures. Under the Demon King's rule, the waterfalls dried up, the Sun didn't shine and the sky was blanketed by grey clouds. Where there had once been flowers, there were now thorny shrubs and vines with dark, sinister blooms. The trees were like skeletons with blackened trunks and few leaves.

The frightened eyes of little creatures peered out from every nook and crevice. They hid from giant snapping lizards, whose teeth glistened with saliva at the prospect of a juicy meal. Full of shadows, there was no beauty or hope.

When the Dark Hearts arrived, their bright manes and jewel-like eyes were dazzling and added a splash of vivid colour in a nightmarish world. They were curious about this strange new place — they had spent so little time in the human world and in some ways the shape of the landscape was not unlike the place they had left. However, their instincts told them to be cautious as they explored their new surroundings.

Using all of their senses to learn as much as they could about their new home, they soon discovered that they could communicate with each other using telepathy.

Broken Horn huffed as one of the smaller Dark Hearts with an indigo-coloured mane and tail, named Blue Lagoon, came alongside him. She nudged him with her nose to comfort him.

"What is worrying you, brother?" she asked.

"We don't belong in this world. I know we had no other choice than to come here, but I feel like it's all my fault. If I hadn't tried to defeat the dragon and put everyone in danger, then we might have been able to stay where we were," replied Broken Horn.

"Don't blame yourself. You tried to help and you meant well. This is our home now so let's explore." Blue Lagoon tossed her mane and cantered forward, curious and brave.

An imp hopped down from one of the trees into her path. Blue Lagoon poked the creature with her nose and it tumbled backwards giving a strange giggle. Five more of its friends flew down from the tree, waving their long, pointed tails from side to side as if to say hello.

Suddenly, a group of fairies swooped in from the branches above and buzzed around the Dark Hearts, taking a good look at them and running their little hands through the unicorns' manes. It seemed to cheer Broken Horn's low spirits and he whinnied softly.

The imps and fairies seemed friendly enough, but there were other creatures lurking all around. Giant black crows perched on branches, their caws loud and angry. Lizards with frills around their necks skittered back and forth on rocks, snapping their teeth at the unicorns' hooves. But the Dark Hearts were not afraid and they kept walking further into the Shadow Realm.

Eventually, they came to a cliff's edge and the land swept down into a dark and dusty crater. A giant creature with scaly green skin sat on a granite throne that had been carved into the side of the cliff. It had horns coming out of the side of its head like a bull. It was the Demon King.

He grinned, flashing a set of sharp, yellowing teeth as he watched small grey trolls scuttle about below. The poor creatures were busy digging, mining and shifting mud into strange shapes and mounds. Their only purpose was to build, chipping away at the ground, digging deeper and deeper.

The Demon King's eyes glimmered as he watched over his domain. If the trolls didn't work fast enough or if they faltered, he pointed a sharp claw at them and struck them with a bolt of lightning, making them writhe in pain.

The Demon King's crater was a dreadful place. The fairies hid behind the Dark Hearts and the imps whimpered quietly.

One of the strange mounds was close to completion. It looked like a Chimera — a creature with the head of a lion, the body of a goat and the tail of a snake. When the last piece went into place, the Demon King struck it with lightning and it came to life. The monstrous creation roared.

Raising a pointed claw into the air, the Demon King made a tear between realms, which led back into the human world. Sunlight and colour burst through the portal, but the Demon King recoiled from the light as it scorched his skin. With his powers weakened by the unicorns' battle with the five-headed dragon, the Demon King was unable to enter the human world. However, he could still create and send monsters there to cause chaos and destruction.

Unaffected, the Chimera was able to pass through and, as soon as it disappeared, the edges of the tear sealed together with a crackling sound. The Shadow Realm was dark once again. The Demon King cracked a whip and the trolls immediately went back to work on another evil creation.

Broken Horn tossed his head, urging his brothers and sisters to move away from the crater.

"What can we do to stop this? It doesn't seem right," he said sadly.

None of the Dark Hearts knew what to say, but they all felt the same. They didn't want to see the trolls suffering, though they hadn't a clue how to stop the Demon King.

The Dark Hearts bowed their heads together in thought, but they were so young and didn't know what their powers could do. Broken Horn had destroyed a mountain, causing a landslide, and the others hadn't even tried to use their magic yet. Who knew what other disasters might happen if they weren't careful? As the unicorns continued to explore the wasteland, the fairies and imps watched them with hope in their eyes. The Dark Hearts wandered for a while longer, but the landscape didn't change.

"We can't carry on much further," said Broken Horn with a sigh. "We're getting tired and hungry."

Most of the Dark Hearts held their heads low to the ground as they walked. Then, Blue Lagoon stamped her hoof to get the group's attention. Something had caught her eye.

"Come with me," she said.

She brought them to the edge of a lake where dark waters foamed and bubbled on its banks. Blue Lagoon waded in slowly and sniffed to see if the water was safe to drink.

Suddenly, the fairies that had followed the Dark Hearts became very agitated and the imps scuttled to hide behind the unicorns. The water started to shift and swirl, but Blue Lagoon stood her ground. Something large that looked like a crocodile emerged and opened its huge jaws ready to gobble her up!

"Look out!" shouted Broken Horn.

Almost the size of three unicorns, the creature had green, bumpy skin and razor-sharp teeth. Blue Lagoon jumped back as the beast's jaws snapped at her hooves. It lashed its tail, whipping it round and sending water flying into the air. Blue Lagoon could see each water droplet briefly hover in the air, reflecting the monster and the rest of the startled Dark Hearts.

Magic crackled from her horn and it was now her turn to see what she could do. She reared up on to her hind legs and slammed her front hooves into the water. The powerful force blasted the creature away and it flew through the air. It squealed before flopping back down into the water. Completely stunned, it swam off as quickly as it could.

Then, a wall of water rose up into the air, shadows and light shimmering over the droplets. Projected on the screen of water, the Dark Hearts could see the Chimera in the human world, but it wasn't alone. The Golden Unicorn was fighting the monster and the Dark Hearts watched as the Chimera was defeated by a beam of magical light coming from the Golden Unicorn's horn.

Once it was over, the sheet of water fell like rain back into the lake. The images disappeared and everything went dark. The Dark Hearts put their heads together, using their psychic powers to discuss what to do.

"If the Golden Unicorn helps to protect people and defeat the Demon King's creations in the human world, then perhaps we might be able to find a way to stop him and free the trolls in the Shadow Realm," said Blue Lagoon excitedly.

Broken Horn huffed. "We need to watch the other unicorns to see how they use their magic. Maybe I can use my magic to make a tear between the realms."

"Go on, try it," said Blue Lagoon.

At first it didn't work and Broken Horn hung his head in despair. Blue Lagoon and the others whinnied softly, encouraging him to try again.

"I can do this!" declared Broken Horn.

After several tries, a stream of light finally spilled out from the sky and into the Shadow Realm. However, unlike the tear the Demon King had created, this one had jagged edges and did not heal itself. The Dark Hearts had created their own portal that they could use to go back into the human world.

Before the others could go through it, Broken Horn stamped his hoof. "Wait. What if instead of helping, we cause more chaos and destruction? We must learn how to use our magic safely, first."

Blue Lagoon was eager to go through, but she huffed in agreement. "You're right, Broken Horn. Let's agree to no magic in the human world until we know what we're doing. Come on, then. We have a lot of work to do!"

She twinkled her eyes mischievously at Broken Horn and leapt through the portal. Broken Horn shook his mane, then cantered after her. The other Dark Hearts, fairies and imps followed, eager to explore and learn.

Friend or Foe?

The Shadow Realm is home to a variety of different creatures.
Some are friends of the Dark Hearts and live alongside them,
while others were created by the Demon King to do his bidding.

FRIENDLY FAIRIES

The fairies in the Shadow Realm
live alongside Dark Hearts, sharing
their food and home. They are all
kinds of colours and their wings
look like those of a butterfly. The
fairies are very communicative and
like to sing, which helps lift the
spirits of the Dark Hearts.

MISCHIEVOUS IMPS

Alongside the fairies live imps,
who are playful and mischievous.
They like to roll and tumble
around like acrobats. Larger than
the fairies, they help Dark Hearts
find kindling for firewood, but
they mostly like to play games.

TROLLS

The Demon King created trolls to serve as his minions.
They build monsters out of mud and rock, which the Demon
King brings to life. They can create anything from werewolves
and dragons to ogres and armies of skeletons. They are skilful
builders, but sad creatures. The Dark Hearts desperately
wish to free them from the Demon King's control.

SNAPPING LIZARDS

Giant snapping lizards lurk in the depths of the lagoons.
They are fearsome creatures with sharp teeth and
swishing tails. The lizards expand their frills to
frighten other creatures and steal their food.

When shadows fell at the Demon King's hand,

Dark Hearts were born to save the land.

The Typhoon
of Terror

This historic sighting was reported in
1755 on the Isle of Skye, Scotland.

"Alastair Macdonald! Stop daydreaming and
get on with your work!" said his mother.
She was waving a piece of fish at him, reminding
him that he was supposed to be fixing
scraps on to the fishing line hooks.

It was five o'clock in the morning and the whole family were getting ready to set sail. Alastair's father, Lachlan, and his Uncle Callum would drag their boat, *The Selkie*, off the beach at Elgol and set out as they had done so many times before. This was the first time Alastair was old enough to go with them.

"We might see an actual kelpie or even the Kraken!" said Alastair. He waved his arms about like an octopus, his eyes wide with excitement. He loved it when his uncle told stories of sea monsters or creatures like kelpies and merfolk.

His sister, Caty, looked up, brushing red curls out of her face. "That's stupid!" she said with a scowl.

"No, it isn't," he said, feeling his cheeks get hot as he blushed with embarrassment.

"You do talk nonsense sometimes, Alastair," said his father with a wink. "The Kraken lives in Norway. It wouldn't come this far south. Get back to the fishing line, son."

Alastair grinned, but did as he was told while listening to his father and uncle discuss where to find the best herring shoals. It was important to get a big catch. It was their livelihood and the family and the village all depended on them selling the fish.

Caty was jealous. She wasn't allowed to go because she was too young. Alastair couldn't help showing his emotion. For as long as he could remember, he'd wanted to be a fisherman like his father and grandfather before him.

Out on the water, the sea was calm and the sky was clear. Gulls followed the boat as it left the beach, their beady eyes ready to steal any caught fish. Alastair sat at the prow, his hair gently flapping in the breeze as he felt the boat rise and fall on the waves of the Hebridean Sea. Uncle Callum pointed out a pod of dolphins.

Apart from a few dark clouds in the west, it was a perfect day. Alastair couldn't believe how lucky he was to finally be at sea. When they came to a good spot, Lachlan and Callum put out the line. Now it was a matter of waiting to see what they caught.

Alastair thought he saw something large in the water. "Look, another dolphin!" he yelled.

His father shaded his eyes against the Sun and looked overboard, but whatever it was it had vanished.

Uncle Callum brought up the line and cried out in shock. They hadn't caught any fish, but all of the bait had disappeared. Lachlan frowned in puzzlement. All of a sudden, the Sun went behind a cloud and the sea turned dark. Then, something hard bumped the boat.

Webbed hands came out of the water and gripped the side of the boat. Alastair staggered backwards as something half-man and half-fish reached out a slimy arm and grabbed him. Lachlan and Callum picked up their oars and struck the creature, forcing it to sink back into the sea.

"What was that?" shouted Lachlan.

"Merfolk!" shrieked Callum.

Alastair cried out as another one tried to snatch at his sleeve from behind. A merman was reaching up and over the side of the boat, trying to grab a hold of him. Lachlan swung the oar round, hitting its head. There was a high-pitched squeal followed by a big splash.

All around them the sea was filled with the bobbing heads of the merfolk, who were determined to drag the fishermen down into the depths. The boat started to rock from side to side as the merfolk tried to capsize it. Lachlan and Callum did their best to fight back, but there were just too many of them.

Suddenly, something black and red whipped past the boat and Alastair thought he heard the soft whinny of a horse. He'd heard the legends about kelpies. They were beautiful, ghostly horses that lured unsuspecting people to drown in deep waters. Alastair spun around to warn his father, but then he stopped. His jaw dropped open in amazement.

Galloping across the water was a unicorn with a black horn
and coat, and a mane as fiery red as his sister's hair — it was
a Dark Heart unicorn. The speed at which it sprinted created
huge, rippling waves, which pushed the merfolk downwards and
away from the boat.

As the wind started to howl, the merfolk disappeared into
the depths. Whatever the unicorn was doing, it had stopped
them, but at the same time it had kicked up the water into a
bewildering white fog. Soon, it was difficult to see at all.

"Get down!" shouted Uncle Callum, over the din of the roaring
waves. Alastair felt his father's hand protectively on his back as
the boat was buffeted about.

The wind was angry, swooping around the boat in terrifying
gusts. A crackling red light emanated from the unicorn's black
horn, turning the white fog red. The water churned and the
rocking of the boat flipped Alastair up into the air and into the
sea. He only just had time to take a big breath.

Under the waves, the sea was like a whirlpool, with ghostly
shapes stirring in the murk. What if the kelpies got him?
Alastair panicked, kicking his legs hard to get to the surface.
Before he knew it, a strong hand grabbed him by his collar and
pulled him out, back on to the deck. Lachlan's worried face
hovered over him. Relieved, they threw their arms around each
other in a hug.

"I thought we'd lost you there for a minute," said Lachlan as he tied a rope around Alastair's waist and secured it to his own belt.

"Dad! There are kelpies under the water!"

"Those aren't kelpies," said Uncle Callum. He pointed and two more unicorns appeared, surfacing from the turbulent sea. "Those are Water Moon unicorns."

Uncle Callum had told him stories about Water Moon unicorns before. With horns glittering like sapphires, these beautiful creatures were graceful and majestic. The Water Moons surrounded the Dark Heart unicorn, whose skittish dance came to an abrupt end.

The water lashed against the sides of the boat, spinning it in dizzying circles. Still, the red mist swirled, carried by the wind at a frightening speed. It was turning into a typhoon.

The Water Moon unicorns tossed their rippling manes, sending streams of blue light from their horns that dispersed the violent sea spray. It worked and the mist disappeared, but it wasn't enough to calm the wind or the sea.

Alastair gripped the rope around his waist and the side of the boat. He wasn't going into the water again. As he looked into the stormy sky two more unicorns appeared. Their coats were as grey as the sky, but their golden manes and tails crackled like lightning.

"Look!" He shouted, pointing to the new unicorns.

"Storm Chasers!" exclaimed Uncle Callum, rubbing his eyes in disbelief.

They joined the other unicorns and used their magic to calm the wind. Together, the Water Moons and the Storm Chasers brought stillness to the sea. As the wind died and the storm came to an end, the skies cleared and the Sun came out. Lachlan and Callum cheered.

Alastair watched the Dark Heart unicorn, which had its head bowed so its nose was almost touching the water. When the other unicorns approached, it turned and bolted across the surface of the sea and away into the west. The Storm Chasers flew after it.

"Begone, dark-hearted one," said Uncle Callum, watching the black-and-red unicorn disappear.

Alastair's father and uncle were too exhausted to row ashore, but the Water Moons stayed with the boat, pushing it back to Skye. They were all safe, but the closer they got to home, the quieter Lachlan and Callum became. Their faces were full of worry. They had failed to catch anything and returning to Elgol with nothing meant that their family and the village would go hungry.

With the island in sight, the Water Moons bowed their heads low as a farewell and retreated back to the open sea. Then, Alastair heard the sound of herring gulls making a racket behind him.

"Dad, why are the gulls so noisy?" he said.

"Quick, Alastair! Help me with the line!" shouted his father.

In all the chaos they had forgotten about the fishing line, but it was still attached to the boat. They hauled it in using all of their remaining strength. Miraculously, after everything they had been through, they had a bountiful catch of herring.

"The unicorns saved our skins today, in more ways than one," said Lachlan.

Wrapped up warm and dry in bed, Alastair recounted the whole story to his sister. Caty listened intently, hanging on to his every word. She was envious of his adventure, but couldn't hide her intrigue.

"Sounds like that black-and-red unicorn was determined to drown you all," she said. Alastair wondered if she was right, but mainly he felt sorry for it.

"I don't think it wanted to cause trouble," replied Alastair. "I think it was trying to save us from the merfolk, but its magic seemed too wild."

"Well, you're lucky to be alive. Next time you go, maybe the Kraken will come." She was half joking, but her eyes looked wistful.

"Maybe you should come next time. Just in case!" said Alastair.

"Do you think Dad will let me?" she asked.

"Aye, I'll make sure he does," he said, smiling fondly at his younger sister.

As his head touched the pillow, Alastair had one last thought before he fell asleep. He hoped that if the Water Moons and Storm Chasers caught up with the Dark Heart, they would not harm it. Later that night he dreamt he was riding the waves with the unicorns, having another maritime adventure.

Spotting a Dark Heart

Dark Hearts were created during a magical eclipse. Perhaps as a result of their mysterious beginnings, they are the most varied of all the unicorn families. Here's what we know about their appearance, distinctive markings and supernatural abilities.

Due to their similarity to Shadow Night unicorns, who also have black coats and horns, it's now believed that some Dark Heart unicorns may have been misidentified in the past.

Their horns are made of black onyx, which symbolizes strength and perseverance.

Each Dark Heart unicorn has a black coat with unique markings.

NOT ALL DARK HEARTS LOOK IDENTICAL

While Dark Hearts have black coats and horns, the colours of
their manes and tails differ. Some are indigo blue, crimson red
or golden yellow. Their coats also have distinctive markings,
which relate to their unique magical abilities. As you may
already know, each unicorn blessing has its own set of
track marks. Below is a Dark Heart's hoof print.

MASTERING THEIR MAGIC

Due to the unpredictable nature of the eclipse, it's taken Dark
Hearts centuries to master their magic. Their supernatural
abilities include making themselves invisible and using their
psychic powers to move things without touching them.

The Dressmaker's Doll

*This encounter was documented
in 1867 in Paris, France.*

Their carriage pulled up at the Paris Opera
House and Hélène and her parents stepped
out. Throngs of wealthy people wearing
fashionable ball gowns, cloaks and tall hats
were arriving to see the ballet that evening.

One of the most celebrated ballet dancers of the time was performing. Hélène's father was the mayor and so they had a family box in the dress circle with a perfect view of the stage. Hélène loved everything about the ballet; the elegant dancers in fantastic costumes, the beautiful music. She often dreamt about becoming a ballerina. While watching the performance, her feet tapped under her skirt, memorizing the steps so that she could practise by herself at home.

After the performance, Hélène got the thrill of her life. Her family were invited backstage to learn more about the production and meet the prima ballerina. Hélène had been desperate to see the sumptuous costumes and scenery up close. While her mother and father spoke at length with the principal dancers in the wings, Hélène wandered about. She marvelled at the painted screens and curtains as the stagehands buzzed around resetting the scenery and props.

"Mind out of the way!" shouted a young man.

He pulled some ropes and one of the backdrops flew into the air above their heads. He frowned at her and tutted, so she apologized and moved along.

Hélène noticed a doorway that led down beneath the stage. Glancing at her parents, she could see they were still deep in conversation with the dancers. She was keen to see the costumes and felt sure they wouldn't notice if she disappeared for a moment.

Hélène ran down the steps as quickly as she could and found herself in a large room. Some of the dancers were seated at tables, removing their shoes and wiping the makeup from their faces. They looked surprised to see Hélène, but smiled politely.

There were no costumes, but she could see a doorway at the end of the dressing room, which she guessed must lead to the wardrobe. She ran past the dancers and went through.

She found a room filled with magnificent costumes from all of the famous ballets and operas. There were Elizabethan costumes with enormous collars and strange medieval masks with big hooked noses. There was also a huge black-and-purple jewelled cloak that reminded Hélène of a raven with long, black feathers. It was so beautiful, she thought, as she traced her fingers over the purple gems admiringly.

At the end of the costume rails was a long worktable. There was a woman with her back turned, busy pinning a costume to a dressmaker's doll. The woman had wild hair and shabby clothes. The mannequin was about Hélène's height and wore a wig of blonde ringlets that were tied up in neat little bows. The dress had a lace bodice and the fabric of the skirt was embroidered with flowers and butterflies, which glimmered in the flickering light of the oil lamps.

The dressmaker turned around as Hélène approached and stared at her with wide eyes, then grinned. Hélène froze. The woman's smile did not seem friendly.

"Hello," said Hélène, trying to be courteous. "What beautiful costumes you have here."

"Made with thread spun from the hair of nosey little girls," the dressmaker replied and before Hélène could think of what to say, the woman reached out and plucked a strand of her hair.

Hélène gave a startled yelp. She turned and hurried back through the costumes. She didn't stop when she came to the dressing room and ran all the way back up the stairs. When she got to the top, she almost ran straight into her parents.

"Wherever have you been?" her mother asked with concern.

Hélène threw her arms around her mother's waist, who gave a puzzled laugh and took hold of her hands. "Are you ready to go home?" she asked. Hélène nodded, too breathless and frightened to speak.

That night, still haunted by the strangeness of the dressmaker, Hélène had a nightmare about the mannequin reaching out to grab her hair. After lying awake for some time, she opened her bedroom window to let in the cool, night-time air and watched the stars twinkling in the moonlit sky.

In the corner of her eye, she thought she saw a bird, but when she looked closer she was astonished to see a magnificent unicorn flying towards her. The creature, a Dawn Spirit unicorn, flew right up to her window and landed on the balcony with the elegance of a dancer. Hélène wondered if she was still dreaming.

The unicorn tossed its head and, without thinking, Hélène climbed out of her window and on to the balcony to meet it. Soon she was combing her fingers through the unicorn's beautiful silky mane, which was the colour of a dawn sky.

The Dawn Spirit bowed its head and Hélène had the strangest feeling that the creature wanted her to climb on to its back. Without hesitating, she lifted herself up and had just enough time to wrap her arms around the unicorn's neck before it flew off the balcony and into the night.

Hélène giggled in delight as the wind whipped through her hair. She felt at ease with the unicorn, her bare toes wiggling in the air, high above the city rooftops. They flew over a park, which lead to the River Seine. The unicorn's hooves skimmed the surface of the water until they came to Notre Dame Cathedral. Then, gliding along a wide road, they passed by the town hall and flew onwards, straight to the Paris Opera House. Without the carriages and opera goers, the square seemed eerily quiet.

Hélène shivered as they approached, anxious at the thought of going back inside. The unicorn whickered softly, as though it understood her fears, and she buried her face into its mane for comfort.

Landing in front of the steps, Hélène caught sight of something moving in the shadows. She heard the soft clump of hooves and realized there was another unicorn. This one's coat was jet black and its mane and tail were the colour of amethyst. It was a Dark Heart unicorn named Raven.

Clearly agitated, Raven was trying to get through the doors to the auditorium, but the Dawn Spirit snorted and stamped its hoof to object, then barged past. To Hélène's surprise, it pushed the door open with its nose and hurried in. Hélène blinked and when her eyes adjusted to the light from the oil lamps, she realized they were not alone.

There was a little girl with golden ringlets standing on the stage, wearing the butterfly costume the dressmaker had made. The girl looked shocked when she saw Hélène riding on the back of the Dawn Spirit unicorn.

"Quickly, help me! I am trapped!" said the girl. "The dressmaker has bewitched me. At dawn, I become a lifeless doll and every night for a few precious hours I come back to life, but I cannot escape. Unless her spell is broken, I'm doomed to stay her prisoner forever."

Suddenly, the Dark Heart unicorn ran past them and leapt
up on to the stage to nuzzle the girl's hand with its nose.

"You came to rescue me," said the girl, stroking Raven's
purple mane.

Somewhere a door banged and the Dark Heart shimmered. One
moment the unicorn was there and the next it was disappearing,
fading against the painted forest backdrop. Then, a long
sinister shadow fell across the stage. Carrying an oil lamp, the
dressmaker stepped out from the wings, her hair wilder than
before. She grabbed the little girl's hand, who screamed.

"Trying to escape, were you? I see you have new friends," she
hissed at Hélène. "I have a strand of your hair — remember!
I can use magic to make you my prisoner, too!"

The air shifted and Raven reappeared in front of the dressmaker
and reared up at her. She fell backwards, dropping the oil lamp
in fright and letting go of the girl. It all happened so quickly. In
almost a flash, the stage curtains had caught on fire.

"Quick!" Hélène waved at the girl, who leapt down from
the stage.

They grabbed each other's hands and ran, not daring to look back until they got to the doors. The Dawn Spirit was approaching the dressmaker who lay in a crumpled heap on the stage, flames dancing around her. As the smoke started to billow into the air, making their eyes water, they had no choice but to run outside. Coughing, it took a moment for them to catch their breath.

"The fire must have broken the spell," said the little girl. "I've never been able to leave the opera house until now."

"What's your name?" asked Hélène.

"Eloise," she replied. Hélène took hold of her hands and smiled. "I'm so glad you're safe."

At that moment the two unicorns burst through the opera's beautiful, historic doors. The Dark Heart was first, then the Dawn Spirit with the dressmaker lying across its back.

The flames were destroying the building. The Dawn Spirit tipped the dressmaker on to the ground and directed an angry snort at Raven, who bowed its head in shame. Hélène wondered if the Dawn Spirit blamed the other unicorn for starting the fire. Perhaps if it hadn't startled the dressmaker, this accident could have been avoided. Hélène felt sad for it and reached out to touch its mane in sympathy, but the unicorn glimmered briefly before fading and disappearing again.

In the distance there were whistles and shouts. The police and the fire brigade were approaching the opera house. Hopefully, they could put out the fire before it caused too much damage.

A wave of tiredness came over Hélène. "I have to go home," she said. The Dawn Spirit neighed softly in agreement.

Eloise looked sad. "I have no home to go to," she said.

"Then come with me. My father is the mayor and we will take care of you," replied Hélène. Eloise's face lit up with joy.

As the sky turned from pink to peach the two girls climbed on to the unicorn's back, leaving the dressmaker lying on the ground. Hélène would tell her father what had happened and he would make sure she was put away for her crimes. Hélène looked for Raven once more, but the unicorn had completely vanished. The Dawn Spirit lifted them into the sky and took them home.

Sometimes in the early mornings, Hélène would remember the Dark Heart who had really tried to help them, but accidentally started the fire. Mostly, she enjoyed reminiscing about flying over the city with Eloise and the Dawn Spirit unicorn.

Broken Horn

Broken Horn is the head of the Dark Heart blessing.
His courage and determination make him a strong leader.

He lost the tip of his horn in a fight with a five-headed dragon.

His black coat has pebble-shaped markings, which reflect his enormous strength and ability to break up large rocks.

Although he is the largest Dark Heart unicorn, he is a gentle giant and light-footed.

Blue Lagoon

This unicorn also leads the Dark Heart family.
She is supportive, tremendously brave and optimistic.

Blue Lagoon has been spotted
all over the world including
Italy, Uruguay and China.

The circles on her
back symbolize her
psychic powers
and her ability to
manipulate water
to reflect events
that happen in the
human world.

She is inquisitive and likes exploring.
The imps and fairies of the Shadow Realm
love to follow her wherever she goes.

Ghosts *of the* Tundra

This sighting was recorded in Alaska in 2010.

Eddie whined softly. "Here you go, buddy," said Kyle, putting some dog food into Eddie's bowl. He grunted appreciatively and started guzzling the food like all the other huskies in the pack.

Kyle gave Eddie a gentle pat on his head and went back into the house, his boots crunching on the snow.

"I fed all the dogs, Mom," said Kyle. His mother, Michelle, was busy making their own dinner in the kitchen.

"Thank you, honey. Time to do your homework. If you get it done quickly, we could take the dogs out for a run after dinner," she said.

Kyle grinned. His mother was a husky musher and ran sledging tours for tourists, but hadn't been running them at night since Kyle's dad had moved away. His parents were getting a divorce and his dad was working as a park ranger in a different town. Kyle still found it hard getting used to the idea that it was just the two of them now, but being out on the ice with the huskies was the best feeling in the world.

After he'd hung up his coat and tugged off his thick boots, Kyle sat down and pulled out a book labelled 'Algebra'. He sighed and started working through the sums, listening to Michelle chopping vegetables. He'd not even got halfway down the page before he realized the dogs were barking outside.

"Mom? Can you hear the dogs?" asked Kyle, going to the window.

"Sounds like something has got them spooked," Michelle said with a frown.

She joined Kyle at the window and looked out into the icy darkness. After a few moments, the dogs fell silent.

"I'm not sure what that was about, but a run tonight will do them good," said Michelle.

By the time Kyle had finished his homework, dinner was ready. While they ate, Michelle talked about the tourists she'd taken out that day with the huskies, people who had come to enjoy the wilderness of Alaska. Kyle talked a bit about some of the things that had happened at school, then he helped clear away the dinner plates while Michelle tidied the kitchen.

They put on their thermals, thick coats and snow boots, before getting the huskies into the harnesses. The always-obedient Eddie let Kyle put his snowshoes on and soon he was stood in the pack with the other six dogs. Margie was the most vocal of the dogs. She was raring to go and Michelle had quite a struggle getting her harness on.

"Did something get you spooked?" Michelle said to her. Margie barked.

Sledding at night was a breathtaking experience. At first, both Kyle and Michelle used the head lamps on their helmets to light the way, but once they'd left the thick cover of the fir trees, there was enough moonlight to guide them. Michelle was leaning left and right, steering the dogs along the track she knew so well. A bubble of excitement rose up in Kyle's tummy; being out in the snow with the dogs was one of his favourite things.

In the distance they could see a snowbank, which would prove a challenge for the dogs to jump over without either Kyle or his mother falling off the sled. But as they got closer, Margie started barking. Soon, the other dogs were barking, too, so Michelle used her brake to slow down. Once they'd come to a stop, she stepped off the sled and secured the anchor. Kyle leaned forward and cooed at Margie to calm her down, but he gasped as something caught his eye in the trees to their right.

Dark shadows were moving and he couldn't work out what he was seeing. Eddie and Margie started snarling, baring their teeth. Then, Kyle's eyes adjusted — it was wolves. But these were no ordinary wolves. They were huge and ferocious, and worst of all they were almost transparent like ghosts.

The sled jerked as the huskies started to run, but they were all trying to pull it in different directions. The huskies dragged it off the track, which skirted the edge of a huge frozen lake. With Margie barking and the others growling, the sled tipped over and Kyle fell out on to the ice.

"Kyle!" Michelle leapt forward to help him.

"Mom, look!" He pointed at the wolves who were advancing with stealth towards them.

"Quick, help me turn over the sled!" his mother shouted.

Kyle pushed himself up and started turning the sled. All of a sudden, the dogs went quiet. They cowered as the wolves crept closer. Kyle trembled. He was terrified.

Suddenly, there was a flash of light and a black unicorn appeared between the dogs and the wolves. Its green tail was luminous in the moonlight and it had markings on its coat, like frost-covered ferns, ethereal and magical. Kyle watched in amazement as the unicorn advanced on the wolves.

The ghostly wolves snapped their vicious teeth at the unicorn as it pointed its horn at them. Sending a stream of purple light at the wolves, like a laser beam, the unicorn drained their power. They howled and Kyle clamped his gloved hands to his ears, gritting his teeth at the horrible gut-wrenching sound. The ghostly energy surged into the unicorn through its horn, but its body started buckling under the pressure and the ice started to crack.

Michelle cried out. They were in terrible danger. Most of the huskies had managed to break free, but Eddie and Margie were still attached and rooted to the spot. The sound of the howling wolves intensified and the ice creaked ominously.

The unicorn reared up and a blast of light exploded from its horn. Kyle knelt down into a crouch and shielded his eyes, unsure what was happening. Suddenly, he heard the ice breaking apart in front of him and without hesitating he stood up, determined to run and save the dogs.

"It's too dangerous, Kyle!" Michelle cried, pulling him back.

Eddie lay spread-eagled on the ice and Margie yelped. The wolves snarled, ready to pounce. Kyle knew that if the wolves got to them, or they fell into the freezing water, the dogs would perish.

Another blast of light shot through the sky and the Northern Lights danced above them. It was unusual to see the phenomenon this far south. Then, two beautiful unicorns appeared. They had to be Ice Wanderer unicorns, thought Kyle. His dad had told him stories about them when he was little. Their thick, white coats sparkled with magic as they glided over the ice, as if they were walking on air. They galloped towards Eddie and Margie to protect them, while the Dark Heart unicorn pursued the wolves. Kyle felt a surge of hope.

The Ice Wanderers used their magic to stabilize the ice so that Michelle and Kyle could drag Margie and Eddie away. The Dark Heart, who Kyle had named Fern Frost, once again tried to suck the ghostly energy from the wolves and it seemed to be working, but an Ice Wanderer kicked up a front hoof as if to object.

In all the chaos and confusion, one of the wolves seized its chance and charged at Kyle, leaping through the air with a snarl in its throat. Fern Frost ran between them and a purple stream of magic crackled from its horn. It snaked out towards the wolf, which dissolved mid-leap in the air. The Ice Wanderers used white jets of magic to destroy the other ghostly wolves and they fizzled, before vanishing.

The sky swirled above their heads in a dazzling display of colour. It struck Kyle that the dancing lights moved in time with the unicorns, like they were communicating with each other. When the wolves had gone, the colourful aurora transformed into a dark, billowing cloud and Kyle had a feeling that the Ice Wanderers were angry with the Dark Heart unicorn.

"I was only trying to help, please believe me," said Fern Frost.

Kyle and Michelle jumped. The voice was loud as if spoken by a person standing right next to them. Although Fern Frost's mouth hadn't moved, Kyle was certain the unicorn was talking to them. How extraordinary, he thought, and glanced at his mother who looked just as amazed.

The Northern Lights above their heads were now broiling black clouds that crackled and burned with sparks of light. Fern Frost dropped his head as if in shame, then turned and bolted into the thick cover of the forest.

"Wait!" shouted Kyle. He reached out a hand to stop the Dark Heart, but it was too late and Fern Frost had disappeared. The dark swirls in the sky immediately returned to the calming greens and blues of the Northern Lights, and the Ice Wanderers seemed peaceful again.

"Did you s-s-see that, Mom? I wanted t-t-to s-say tha-thank you. It s-saved our lives!" said Kyle, through chattering teeth.

"I did, it was incredible. Come on, we better get you home before you freeze," Michelle said, securing Margie and Eddie's harnesses to the rest of the team.

The dogs bristled with nervous excitement and did not seem afraid of the Ice Wanderers. One of the unicorns stepped forward and nuzzled Kyle's hand with its nose and he immediately stopped shivering. Kyle giggled, feeling its warmth ripple through his skin and all the way down to his frozen toes.

"Thank you for protecting us," he said and the unicorn snorted softly.

After the Ice Wanderers had galloped away, his mother turned the sled around.

"I've seen a lot of things out here in the wilderness, but I never thought I'd see unicorns," said Michelle with a smile. Eddie gave a friendly bark of approval.

When they got home, they talked over hot chocolate and cookies by the fire about what they had seen that evening.

"Is it too late to call Dad and tell him about the unicorns?" asked Kyle.

"No, I think he will be very interested to hear about this," said Michelle thoughtfully. "Go ahead. Just a quick call, then bed."

Kyle told his dad about the Ice Wanderers and the Dark Heart unicorn. A few days later, his dad helped him make a report of his findings to give to the MUS and it was confirmed as an exceptionally rare sighting. Since that day, Kyle has often wished he might see Fern Frost once more so that he can thank the unicorn properly for saving their lives on the ice.

When darkness lingers day and night,

Unicorn magic brings hope and light.

Red Mist

This Dark Heart is fierce and resilient.
She loves racing across rivers, lakes and oceans.

Red Mist is able to transform into other magical creatures.

Parallel wavy lines mark her coat, which reflect her ability to navigate stormy seas and surf huge waves.

She is one of the fastest Dark Hearts and is able to run effortlessly across water, just like Water Moon unicorns.

Raven

Raven is kind and empathetic. She is quick to sense when other animals and humans are in danger or distress.

Shy and elusive, Raven was first spotted in Paris, France.

Raven can detect animals and humans in need of her help from thousands of miles away.

She can camouflage herself to blend in with her surroundings, making her totally invisible.

The Unicorns
and the Spider

This encounter was recorded in
1395 in Cornwall, England.

Amelia pulled back her bow and released
an arrow. She missed her target
and the lucky hare sprang across
the field, away into the hedgerow.

"No luck today," she said with a sigh. She knew she needed more practice.

Amelia's younger brother, Martin, came to join her, his mouth smeared red with juice. He held up his tiny cupped hands to offer her some wild strawberries.

"Where did you find those?" she asked, popping one in her mouth.

"By the orchard," said Martin, gesturing back the way he had come.

"First one there gets to eat them all!" she said with a giggle and started running. She was determined to get there before him, but suddenly she heard their names being called in the distance.

"Amelia! Martin!" It was their mother.

As they came over the rise towards the manor, they could see her beckoning them from outside the thick walls. She was cross as there was work to be done. Amelia gave her brother a solemn look.

"Let's run back and eat all the strawberries later," she said. He grinned and they both trudged towards the grand towers of their home, passing through the flower-filled garden. Flags with their family crest flapped in the wind; a magnificent unicorn with a golden horn surrounded by twisting stems and rosebuds. Their family was well respected in the area, governing the land and farms in the neighbouring hills.

Inside the manor house everyone was busy preparing for a banquet. Amelia and Martin followed their mother, skipping behind her through the kitchens where cooks and servants were busy preparing enormous stews, tarts and pies.

Amelia was now old enough to help her mother arrange the table in the Great Hall, while Martin was kept out of mischief playing with sticks. He watched Amelia, his mother and the other servants set out huge platters of meat, fruit and vegetables on the long table in preparation for the feast. When they had finished, as promised, Amelia took her brother back to the orchard.

"Show me where you found them?" she asked.

"Here. They were here," he said, running over to a patch in the ground.

When Amelia joined him, she found a blackened tangle of leaves, but there were no strawberries. They hunted around the orchard, but no matter how hard they tried they couldn't find the strawberries anywhere.

"Perhaps the birds or field mice have eaten them," said Amelia, touching his shoulder kindly, but he frowned and shook his head.

The Sun was setting and Amelia felt a chill in the air. As they walked back to the house something moving in the shadows caught her eye.

Amelia's mouth dropped open as she realized it was the swishing tail of a unicorn. It had a series of markings on its coat that reminded Amelia of the vines that sprawled up the side of their house. She tugged her brother's sleeve and they watched as the unicorn bowed its head to sniff the ground. It seemed to be looking for something. Then, a sharp screech sent a shiver down Amelia's spine, startling the unicorn, who bolted into the woods. Grabbing Martin's hand, they hurried back home.

The following day, while Amelia and Martin were playing a game of draughts, there was a commotion in the courtyard. Their father was leaving on horseback with his squire.

"Where is he going, Mother?" Amelia asked, curious about the hurried way in which he'd left the manor. Whenever he went away, he always said goodbye first.

"There's a blight destroying crops in the wheat fields. He's going to see how badly they've been affected," said her mother with a worried look.

Amelia heard the servants whispering. "If there's no grain, there'll be no pies, no bread and no cake. People will starve," said the cook, putting her hands to her mouth with fear.

Martin was too young to understand and pestered his sister to go back to the orchard to see if they could find the strawberries. Even though Amelia knew better, she decided they would go and investigate. She secretly hoped they might see the unicorn again.

When they arrived at the orchard they found the gardener staring at the trees with a dismayed expression on his face. All of the branches were blackened and had dropped their leaves. The fruits were withered and rotting when only yesterday they had been plump and ripening.

"What's happened?" asked Amelia, stunned.

"It's the blight. It's reached us already. I had better send word to your father," he said, leaving with a sad shake of his head.

Huge grey clouds passed overhead, casting shadows over the orchard. Just when they thought things couldn't get any worse, a storm was coming. The wind tugged at Amelia's hair and she quivered. Leaves swirled in the air above them as the sky grew dark. All of a sudden, the shadows merged into the shape of a huge spider the size of a bull. Clicking its sharp pincers, it crawled towards them.

Amelia screamed and grabbed Martin by the arm, dragging him backwards and out of the creature's path. But the spider only had eyes for the vegetable garden. They watched in horror as the monster wove a web over the entire plot. The silvery web crackled with a sinister green light and everything underneath it withered instantly. The spider snapped its pincers — it wanted more.

"Run!" Amelia shouted, pulling Martin's arm back up the slope. When they arrived at the manor Amelia tried to tell her mother what had happened.

"You're imagining things!" she said with a sigh. Even after they'd taken her to the destroyed vegetable beds she still shook her head. "This is serious indeed, but a giant spider did not do this. What nonsense! It's the blight, not a monster from nightmares. Both of you, go straight to bed!"

On the way up to their bedrooms Amelia passed a huge tapestry showing a hunting expedition in the forest. A beautiful unicorn with flowers in its mane and tail stood majestically watching over the hunt. It helped to banish the memory of the monstrous creature's eight staring eyes and it gave her courage. Running to her bedside, she pulled out a box from under the bed. Inside was a small carved statue of a Woodland Flower unicorn. She clutched it to her chest and made a wish.

"Woodland Flowers, please hear our pleas, and banish the blight from the orchard trees." Feeling hopeful, she fell asleep with the toy in her arms.

In the early hours of the morning, she suddenly awoke to the sound of a gentle, high-pitched neigh. Her heart fluttered as she wondered what to do. She tiptoed across the wooden floorboards following the sound downstairs. There, she found a Woodland Flower unicorn standing in the hall and the smell of the roses in its mane and tail filled the room.

Like a thought placed inside her head, Amelia heard the unicorn speak to her. "Stay close to me," it said. "I will protect you."

She followed the unicorn down into the cellar where the food was kept, but a clicking sound made her freeze in terror. Lurking behind barrels of cured meat the spider unfolded its legs and rose up so that its head touched the low ceiling. The Woodland Flower thumped a hoof on the stone floor and the spider hissed at them threateningly. The unicorn kicked out its front legs to attack, but the monster snapped its pincers and released a silvery web, ensnaring the unicorn completely.

The Woodland Flower shook its mane as it tried to untangle itself from the web, but it had been weakened by the trap and slumped to the ground. The spider made a chittering sound ready to attack again, only this time Amelia would be the target. Despite the risk to her own life she rushed to the unicorn with tears in her eyes. Suddenly, there was a flash of light and a second, larger unicorn appeared before them. Amelia recognized it as the unicorn she'd seen in the orchard the day before. Even in the darkness, its eyes sparkled like diamonds.

"I am Blackthorn, a Dark Heart unicorn. This creature does not belong here and I am here to stop it," its defiant voice echoed inside Amelia's head.

An aura of purple light shone out from Blackthorn's horn and the web covering the Woodland Flower began to crackle and dissolve. Then, the Dark Heart turned to the spider and lowered its horn, aiming its magic at the beast. The spider jumped out from behind the barrels, ready to spring, but was struck by the jet of light from the unicorn's horn.

The hideous creature fell backwards, screeching. To Amelia's surprise, the spider started shrinking and soon enough it had shrunk to the size of a normal spider. Blackthorn raised its horn, levitating what was left of the beast into the air. A strange light sparkled over it and it disappeared in a flash.

"Are we safe?" Amelia asked with concern.

"I have sent the spider back to where it belongs and it can do no more harm," said Blackthorn reassuringly.

"Thank you," Amelia said, smiling with gratitude.

Tossing its mane, Blackthorn leapt up the wooden steps out of the cellar. The Woodland Flower unicorn nuzzled Amelia, encouraging her to climb on to its back and they followed.

Outside, the Moon was shining high above the orchard. A lump formed in Amelia's throat as she stared at the blackened trees of the orchard. She touched the scorched leaves of the strawberry patch and they crumbled between her fingers. The two unicorns snorted softly beside her, then the Woodland Flower bowed its head to the ground. Buds started to swell on the leafless trees and tiny shoots began to emerge from the soil. Blackthorn watched the Woodland Flower unicorn carefully, then copied it. Amazingly, the plants grew twice as big as they had been before and little white flowers blossomed. Amelia threw her arms around Blackthorn's neck. All around them, life was returning to the garden.

At dawn, Amelia woke up back in her bed, but she couldn't remember how she'd got there. Had she been dreaming? She had to see for herself to be sure.

She woke up her brother and they ran down to the orchard. Amelia felt hot tears of relief as she saw the trees now in full leaf once again as if the blight and the spider had never existed. Martin tugged her skirt. He was pointing to a clump of red strawberries nearby.

"First one there gets to eat them all!" she laughed and they raced over to them.

With the damaged fields revived, she knew it was all thanks to the unicorns. As Martin and Amelia grew older, they would sometimes see the two unicorns galloping together across the fields. It was clear that they'd become friends and their magic protected the land. When Amelia became the Lady of the Manor, she made sure that a symbol of the Dark Heart unicorn joined the Woodland Flower unicorn on their family crest to signify prosperity and fruitfulness. Together, they had made the spider disappear and ended the blight, and Amelia would always be grateful to them.

Fern Frost

This Dark Heart is wise and quick-witted. He thrives in high altitudes and in cold, brutal temperatures.

Luminous fern fronds decorate his coat, which represents his love for colder climates.

He can use his psychic powers to move any object with his mind.

His favourite food is spring-flowering crocus, a goblet-shaped flower with a light scent

Blackthorn

Blackthorn is the Dark Heart most in tune with nature.
He is a sociable unicorn and has a deep affinity
with animals of other species.

The markings on his coat look
like green, thorn-shaped vines,
which reflect his ability to
accelerate plant growth.

He was first spotted in Cornwall,
England, and has since been
seen in Spain and Australia.

Blackthorn is very good at finding sources of
food. He can also use his magic to grow crops
to feed other creatures in the Shadow Realm.

Adventure *in the* Atlas Mountains

Written by Indira Jenkins using field trip research.

Addam pointed to a ridge above our heads. "Indira, look!" he said.

Lifting my binoculars, I could see a horned sheep jumping from rock to rock. I smiled; the rugged terrain of the mountains and the animals that lived in these desert-like conditions were so fascinating.

Omar, Addam's father, had stumbled across some stone tablets while hiking in the Atlas Mountains in Morocco. The artefacts were covered in symbols that depicted Dark Heart unicorns. When he got in touch with the MUS to report his findings and Uncle Selwyn heard about the discovery, Omar suggested that they organize an expedition to the area. The idea was to gather as much information as possible, but to also make a holiday of it. Besides translating the tablets, Uncle Selwyn was working with Omar to create a purpose-built museum for them in Marrakesh, which would attract visitors from all over the world.

My parents stayed at the village of Imlil, busy analyzing the symbols to better understand the origins of the Dark Hearts, while Uncle Selwyn and I leapt at the chance to see one of these rare, largely undocumented unicorns in the wild. Uncle Selwyn and I left with Omar and Addam in the evening. I was nervous about navigating our way up the mountains while it got dark, but Omar insisted that it was better to see the unicorns at night.

"Come this way," Omar said, taking us further up the mountain track. "There's a plateau just over that ridge and with any luck we'll see something more exciting than a mountain sheep."

Eventually, we came to the plateau and the view was stunning with the Sun setting behind the peaks in the west. I took lots of pictures on my phone, including a selfie with Addam.

I was so busy looking around that I nearly tripped over what I thought was a rock. Bending down, I found a very unusual cone-shaped fossil that was caked in powdery deposits. I decided to put it in my satchel and take it to my parents. They would know the best way to clean and preserve it.

When I looked up, Uncle Selwyn was pointing into the distance. I followed his finger and to my surprise two magnificent unicorns were galloping across the mountains. I couldn't believe that I was finally seeing not one, but two unicorns. They were breathtaking. One unicorn had a coat the colour of warm copper with a twisting, bronze horn, while the other had a silvery grey coat and a horn made of coral.

"Can you identify them, Indira?" asked Uncle Selwyn with a smile.

"I think the one with the grey coat must be a Mountain Jewel and the coppery one is a Desert Flame," I said, grinning.

"It's unusual to see two different unicorn families together like this," said Uncle Selwyn. "It's fascinating, in fact."

I quickly forgot my worries about the encroaching darkness and to my astonishment the unicorns came close enough to touch. It was the first time I had ever seen a unicorn and I had never imagined I would get to touch one, too. We watched them play together for a while, but as soon as the Sun had set behind the jagged peaks my fears about our safety returned.

"Should we return to the village now?" I asked anxiously.

"We haven't seen a Dark Heart yet. Let's stay a bit longer," said Omar.

Just as the last remaining light disappeared on the horizon, we finally got what we were hoping for. Almost appearing out of thin air, a Dark Heart leapt towards its unicorn cousins.

"I call this one Shadow Star," said Addam and I could see why. Its mane and tail were the colour of turquoise and its black coat was dappled with star-shaped markings.

The most amazing thing was that the Mountain Jewel and the Desert Flame went to greet the Dark Heart, before frolicking together and racing around the plain like old friends. Shadow Star didn't come near us at first, but soon curiosity got the better of it and it cantered over. It snorted softly and shook its tail playfully. I waited patiently and eventually Shadow Star let me stroke its mane.

"As much as I'm enjoying seeing the unicorns, we should get back to the village now," said Uncle Selwyn.

Omar nodded, but Addam's face mirrored mine. Neither of us were ready to go. Reluctantly, Addam called out to the unicorns to say goodbye and then I realized why Omar had said it was better to see the unicorns at night. Our faces were suddenly aglow, reflecting the unicorn magic.

"I will guide you back to the village. There is danger around," said a female voice speaking inside my head. Addam and Omar smiled at us and nodded, and then it slowly dawned on me. It was Shadow Star's voice.

"My word," said Uncle Selwyn, "It seems our Dark Heart friend has strong telepathy skills." We could all hear her voice.

To my surprise, the Desert Flame lowered its head and allowed Addam and his father to climb up on its back. The Mountain Jewel did the same, inviting both me and Uncle Selwyn to climb up. Shadow Star led the way safely down the mountainside back to the village, trotting effortlessly down the steep slope. As we descended I had the strangest feeling that we were being watched, but no matter how hard I peered into the darkness I couldn't see anything.

Over the next few days, we got to know the three unicorns very well, travelling up the mountainside at dusk to study them further. My parents even came a few times to see this extraordinary unicorn behaviour for themselves. Eventually, Uncle Selwyn and Omar allowed Addam and I to travel alone, satisfied that the unicorns would bring us safely home each night. Being with the unicorns was the most wonderful experience. Shadow Star was our interpreter and through her we got to know so much about them. They were all quite young unicorns, and enjoyed racing and playing together.

"Come with us, we want to show you more of our world," said Shadow Star one night. The Desert Flame gave an encouraging nuzzle and the Mountain Jewel tossed its mane approvingly, but I was unsure.

"Perhaps we ought to go back," I said, concerned.

"Let's just have a quick look, please?" asked Addam, with big imploring eyes.

"I suppose we could go a little bit further," I replied.

The unicorns took us along a jagged mountain ridge. On the eastern side the sky was indigo, twinkling with the Evening Star, while the west side was still the deep orange-red of sunset. As we travelled further I noticed the dark shadow of a mountain peak, or so I thought. As we came closer, I could see the silhouettes of three creatures, one large and two smaller. The Desert Flame snorted and Shadow Star thumped her hooves on the ground, but they continued moving closer towards the dark shapes.

Suddenly, my eyes adjusted and I could see a macaque monkey and its babies. They were shrieking, but I quickly realized that we were not the cause of their distress. There was something else lurking in the shadows, but it was so dark I couldn't make it out. The Mountain Jewel's horn shone brightly, but the black shadow seemed to grow darker.

Then, out of the darkness, a huge, angry bear appeared. It bared its sharp teeth, which were dripping with saliva. It roared and the macaque wrapped its arms around its babies, its teeth exposed in a snarl.

"We need to go back, now!" I called.

Addam was alarmed, but he hesitated. "What about the macaques?"

"I will take care of them," said Shadow Star defiantly.

The Mountain Jewel snorted again and beat a hoof on the ground. The Desert Flame whinnied in response and nudged us with its nose to move further back. Suddenly, the bear charged towards the macaque and its babies. Shadow Star leapt forward to challenge the beast, its horn ablaze with light. With the bear distracted, the macaque scooped up its babies and retreated into the darkness. The unicorn's magic was clearly working, but the bear changed direction and started to move towards us. The other two unicorns added their own magic to the fight and soon they all had the bear surrounded.

"We're winning," breathed Addam.

But suddenly the bear reared up and somehow it was larger than before. Its threatening claws were ready to strike. The Mountain Jewel leapt in front of the bear, but the huge monster swiped it out of the way and ran straight at us.

"No!" I screamed.

Addam grabbed my hand tightly. We were frozen to the spot and both knew that there was no way we could outrun this beast.

Shadow Star stood on her hind legs and a beam of purple light shot from her horn, hitting the bear's enormous body. In an instant, the creature began to twist into a nightmarish swirl of shadows, before breaking apart and disappearing into the air like smoke.

Shadow Star and the Desert Flame galloped towards the Mountain Jewel, who was lying on its side. It was badly hurt, but the other two unicorns put their glowing horns together and within moments it was back on its feet. The three unicorns took us home and this was the first time that Shadow Star let us ride on her back. The Dark Heart's star-shaped markings gleamed in the darkness as we travelled down the mountainside.

Back at the village, once the initial panic for our safe return was over, Uncle Selwyn, Omar and my parents listened to our story with great interest.

"Did you say a light emitted from Shadow Star's horn?" asked my mum.

"Yes, and the bear changed shape," I replied.

"The bear was not of this world. It was a beast of shadows," said Addam with a frown.

"How intriguing," said Uncle Selwyn, wrinkling his nose in thought.

"Yes. I wonder if there's anything in the stone tablets that can tell us more," said my dad, pushing his glasses back on to his nose and rummaging through his notes.

"Not tonight. It's very late and you both must be exhausted," said my mum. "Let's get you to bed."

As I settled down to sleep that night I couldn't stop thinking about how well the unicorns had worked together as a team. It had taken all three of them to stop the monstrous bear and none of them could have done it alone. I shivered at the thought of the shadowy beast, but was inspired by the courage and friendship of the unicorns.

No time to waste when there are worlds to save,
Friendship and teamwork make unicorns brave.

Shadow Star

Shadow Star is loyal and protective. She is a trusted friend to all of the other Dark Hearts.

Sociable and free-spirited, she is best friends with a Dawn Spirit and Desert Flame unicorn.

She is the most lively Dark Heart and loves playing games with the other unicorns.

Her favourite food is Rock Jasmine, a flower found in mountainous regions.

Ember

This unicorn is a beacon of light for all of the other Dark Hearts.
He is encouraging, positive and helps to guide those in need.

He has developed the skill
of levitation, meaning he can
make himself and other things
fly, which comes in handy
when there is danger.

His long silky mane is very
popular with the fairies in
the Shadow Realm, who like
to snuggle inside it.

Ember can make sparks with his hooves to light
campfires in the cold, dark world of the Shadow Realm.

The Battle *for the* Shadow Realm

Written by Indira Jenkins using field trip research.

On a recent trip to Morocco I had found what I thought was a fossil. It reminded me of a unicorn horn and so I had brought it in to the MUS library for further investigation.

The cone-shaped fossil certainly looked like a horn, but was covered in sludge. While I was at the library, an expert cleaned away the mud and sand to reveal a broken, black onyx horn. We were amazed at what we saw and wondered what secrets it might hold.

When I fell asleep that night, I dreamt I was in the library again walking alongside a beautiful Shadow Night unicorn. Not unlike a Dark Heart, its black coat was peppered with stars and its silvery mane gleamed as we walked between the tall shelves.

"Can you find the horn from the Atlas Mountains?" asked the unicorn.

"Yes, of course!" I said, going to the artefact desk where I'd left it.

Smiling, I picked up the horn and the Shadow Night unicorn whinnied softly.

"Use it to create a tear between worlds. Then take it to the Dark Heart unicorn called Broken Horn. It's a matter of life and death."

I jumped awake thinking it was just a dream, but I could feel something heavy lying on the end of the bed near my feet. I ran my fingers over the smooth, cold object and could feel it was the broken horn.

Thoughts buzzed around in my head. How did it get here? What did the Shadow Night mean by 'make a tear between worlds' and 'it's a matter of life and death'? My heartbeat raced inside my chest.

Strangely, the horn seemed to grow warm in my hands. Pretending to hold it like a wand, I smiled and drew a spiral in the air, but it suddenly began to glow green and I nearly dropped it in fright. To my amazement, the wall of my bedroom parted like a curtain. Even though it was still night-time, bright light poured through the crack and a blast of cold air hit my face.

My stomach flipped over. It didn't feel like a dream, so, taking a deep breath to steady my nerves, I put on my slippers and a hoodie, and walked through the tear.

All of a sudden, I found myself on a desolate mountainside. Gnarled, blackened trees and boulders stretched for miles below me. I decided this adventure was a terrible idea and turned to go back through the tear, but to my horror the gap in the wall had disappeared. I was trapped.

Unsure what to do next I turned to walk along the narrow path, but I tripped and fell. I expected to slam on to the ground, but I didn't. I felt weightless, like being on a swing. I opened my eyes to find I was floating through the air.

At the foot of the mountainside was a Dark Heart unicorn, shining with a magical purple glow. It whinnied softly as I landed gently next to it.

"My name is Ember. How did you get here? The Shadow Realm is no place for humans. You should be careful."

"I found this," I said, showing Ember the broken horn. "A Shadow Night told me I had to bring it to Broken Horn."

Ember huffed. "Astonishing! Yes, I can see why — the broken horn belongs to him. It was chipped off when we were banished to this realm centuries ago and it's been lost ever since. Climb on my back and I will take you to find him."

As Ember galloped across the rocky plain a little bird landed on my shoulder, but when I looked closer I was stunned to see the smiling face of a fairy. It chattered in a language I didn't understand.

We rode on until we came to the edge of a vast crater. The fairy whimpered and hid itself in Ember's mane. Below, a procession of trolls were digging and building, and my chest tightened as I made sense of what I could see. What I'd mistaken for a ginormous statue was actually a monster, with scaly, green skin and two horns sprouting from its head.

"That is the Demon King," said Ember, reading my mind.

"We need all of the unicorn blessings to help us defeat him and free the creatures under his control. However, while Dark Hearts can move between realms freely, without the magic from that broken piece of horn, the other blessings cannot come here," Ember said, sorrowfully.

"But now you have the horn, which can tear portals between worlds," I said, lifting it up with a smile.

With the sound of thundering hooves, a herd of Dark Hearts joined us at the crater's edge. One Dark Heart stood out to me. Unlike the others, his horn had a jagged edge. This had to be the unicorn I was meant to find.

"You must be Broken Horn. My name is Indira. I have something for you." I dismounted and presented the onyx horn, and he tossed his head in shock.

"Wherever did you find that?" he asked.

"In the Atlas Mountains. I believe it's yours." He bowed his head to show me the jagged stump and I carefully put the horn in place. There was a blinding flash of light as the two pieces of horn hissed and joined together. There was still a hairline crack along the horn, but the break had healed.

"Thank you for finding this," Broken Horn said with a gentle snort. "My magic feels stronger now. Come, my Dark Heart brothers and sisters. Let us try to defeat the Demon King, once and for all. Indira, you must stay here out of harm's way."

As one, the Dark Hearts moved into a line and galloped down into the crater. I watched from a distance as the trolls stopped working and moved aside for the unicorns. The Demon King stood up from his mountainous throne and Broken Horn and the other Dark Hearts formed a semi-circle in front of him. They aimed their horns at him and magical blue light burst into the air. The Demon King snarled and uncurled a sharp talon from his fist, sending lightning bolts to blast the unicorn magic into nothing.

Broken Horn reared up on his hind legs in a silent command and all the Dark Hearts tried once again to use their magic against the Demon King. Around me, several fairies and imps had come to join us. A quiet hope burned in their eyes. The trolls in the crater were all watching, too, and knew their lives depended on the outcome of this battle.

The Demon King took in a huge breath and roared. Lightning surged from his claws with such force that I was momentarily blinded and then everything went dark. I held my breath, waiting for my eyes to adjust.

A cold, horrible laugh cut through the silence that followed. "Ha! You cannot defeat me!" growled the Demon King.

The drumming of hooves announced the Dark Hearts' return to the crater's edge. They were thankfully unharmed. Ember came to join me and nudged my hand with his nose.

Broken Horn snorted. "Our magic isn't strong enough. He's too powerful."

"We must ask our cousins to help," said Ember. "We can prove that we are no longer a danger because we have finally mastered our powers, so they can join forces with us."

Broken Horn bowed his head and the other Dark Hearts touched their horns to his. The air rippled around us as they used their magic to summon the other blessings. Suddenly, over a hundred tears appeared in the sky like doorways and through each one came a unicorn.

Not all of the unicorns looked pleased to be there. A group of Ice Wanderers stamped their hooves in anger. Then two of the most striking unicorns came forward, the Golden and Silver Unicorns — the first unicorns the world had ever known.

"Why have you summoned us here, Broken Horn? This is not our world," said the Golden Unicorn.

"We swear to you that we have learned to master our skills. Now, we need your help to defeat the Demon King," said Broken Horn.

The Silver Unicorn looked around and neighed in agreement. "If we work together we could succeed. Nature must be restored to this land."

The Golden Unicorn bowed its head and moved to the edge of the crater. All of the unicorns followed and when the Golden Unicorn whinnied and stood on its back legs, the other blessings prepared to attack.

The Demon King got to his feet, towering above the unicorns. Pressing his palms together he created a magical ball of fire. He hurled it at the unicorns and I clutched my hands to my face, too afraid to watch. The Ice Wanderers cast up an icy shield and the Water Moons sent water to quench the flames. All of the other unicorns bowed their heads and blasted jets of light at the Demon King to weaken him, while the Dark Hearts added their own glowing magic into the beams.

Suddenly, the mounds near the trolls began to judder and the heaps of earth transformed into mud monsters. They lunged at the first line of unicorns, swiping them with their huge fists. Some of the Dark Hearts moved to attack the creatures using their special magic, and Woodland Flower and Shadow Night unicorns joined them.

The Storm Chasers and Dawn Spirits attacked from the skies, while the Mountain Jewels and Desert Flames charged up the steep mountain to attack the Demon King from behind.

Slowly but surely, the combined magic of all of the unicorns weakened the Demon King. He writhed and growled, and green energy seeped out of his body and passed into the Dark Hearts. Finally, he started shrinking, until he was no bigger than a mortal man. Stunned, he reached up to feel that the horns on his head had vanished, then he slumped to his knees — a Demon King no more.

As the evil magic crackled harmlessly into the ground the mud monsters crumbled to dust. All of the unicorns neighed in a victory cheer. The man wept with relief, grateful to be free from the wicked curse and finally human again.

Suddenly, a cascade of water burst from the top of the mountain into a waterfall, sending a fine mist out into the air. As the mist touched the trolls in the crater, they changed from dull, grey creatures into colourful cheering ones. Grass and flowers burst into life as if it was springtime, and the barren land bloomed once more.

Together with the fairies and imps, the trolls thanked all of the unicorns for uniting and saving their world, but especially the Dark Hearts for finding a way to help them. The Golden and Silver Unicorns led the other blessings in a bow to honour the Dark Hearts, too. All of unicorn-kind was now united in peace.

Ember came to find me. "It's time to take you home, Indira."

I nodded, but before I went, Broken Horn and all the Dark Hearts came to say thank you and goodbye. All around us, the Shadow Realm was changing into a beautiful and vibrant world.

When I woke in the morning it all felt like a dream. Bleary eyed, I touched my dusty hair and could see my slippers were dirty, too. It had to have been real, I thought as I hurried to tell my parents what I had seen. I had flown through the air, met friendly fairies and seen an epic battle between all of the unicorns and the Demon King. But most of all, I would never forget seeing the Dark Hearts master their magic and save the day.

Where in the World?

Broken Horn

Blue Lagoon

Red Mist

Raven

Fern Frost

Blackthorn

Shadow Star

Ember

Arctic Ocean

North America

Pacific Ocean

Atlantic Ocean

South America

Since their creation, the Dark Hearts have wandered far and wide. This map shows some of the known locations where our Dark Heart friends have turned up.

Asia

Europe

Africa

Pacific Ocean

Indian Ocean

Australia and Oceania

Southern Ocean

WHICH DARK HEART ARE YOU?

Just like unicorns, everyone has a unique personality, and we all have different qualities and strengths. Find out which Dark Heart unicorn best represents you by answering these questions, then find out what that means on the following page.

Find a quiet place to sit down with them so that they can talk about how they're feeling.

A day spent indoors doing arts and crafts with your friends.

One of your friends is feeling sad. How do you help them?

Find an adventure to take their mind off it.

START
What would be your perfect day?

Quickly stop to give them a hint and then carry on to ace the rest!

A day spent outside playing games and doing fun team challenges.

Another team is struggling with one of the challenges. What do you do?

Ask them if they'd like to join your team — the more the merrier!

Would you rather sit around a campfire or plant some seeds?

Sit around a campfire: there's nothing like a warm glow to make memories.

EMBER

Plant seeds: digging is relaxing, plus you get to make things grow.

BLACKTHORN

Do you prefer to tell ghost stories or play practical jokes on people?

Tell ghost stories: it's fun being mysterious.

BLUE LAGOON

Play practical jokes: you love being mischievous!

SHADOW STAR

It's time for the next adventure. What will it be?

Tree climbing: you're lightfooted with a great sense of balance.

BROKEN HORN

A water park: you love nothing more than swimming and splashing!

RED MIST

If you could be an explorer, where would you rather go?

The North or South Pole: you love snow and ice.

FERN FROST

The jungle: you're great at camouflage, allowing you to see loads of animals.

RAVEN

BROKEN HORN

Bold and courageous, Broken Horn is
a great leader. He is determined and
found a way to use his magic even
after losing part of his horn.

BLUE LAGOON

Blue Lagoon is a keen
explorer and always up for
investigating any mysteries.

RED MIST

The fastest Dark Heart, Red Mist
loves racing across water and
exploring the ocean.

RAVEN

Kind and empathetic, Raven can sense from
thousands of miles away when humans and
other animals are in need of her help.

FERN FROST

Fern Frost has to be tough to live in
the frozen north, but loves playing in
the snow with the Arctic animals.

BLACKTHORN

Protector of plants and wildlife,
Blackthorn has a deep love for nature.
His special power is growing crops
to provide for those in need.

SHADOW STAR

Lively and adventurous, Shadow Star is
the most daring of the Dark Hearts. She's
mischievous, too, and loves playing games.

EMBER

Positive and encouraging, Ember is a
beacon of hope for all the Dark Hearts.
His ability to light campfires helps
keep his family warm.

The Spotter's Guide to Finding Unicorns

Here is some useful information to help you find a unicorn.

TIME OF DAY

Dark Hearts have been spotted at different times of the day and night, but most sightings usually occur at dusk. We think this is because they are drawn to the eclipse-like conditions in which they were created, when there was very little light.

NATURAL PHENOMENON

You are more likely to see any type of unicorn during the occurence of a rainbow or thunderstorm. Sightings are also more likely during a full or new Moon.

EQUIPMENT

• Binoculars are a must as it's not always possible to get close to these shy creatures.

• Always bring a snack. Spotting a unicorn requires lots of waiting around and you might get hungry!

Remember to be patient. Unicorns are rare and hard to find, so don't be disheartened if you don't see one on your first expedition.

Joining the Society

Now it's up to you to continue the great work of
the Magical Unicorn Society. As you have seen,
anyone can have an encounter with a unicorn
and it often happens when it's least expected.

Why not become a member of the Magical Unicorn Society?
The first step is to memorize the Society's special oath:

By the magical strength of the Mountain Jewel,
And the heart of the Woodland Flower,
By the speed of the dashing Desert Flame,
By hooves, by horns, by power.

I swear to hold the secret close,
To protect unicorns of every variety.
I am proud to be an enchanted member
of the Magical Unicorn Society!

Then, visit our website and follow the instructions:

www.magicalunicornsociety.co.uk
#MagicalUnicornSociety

Good luck, and happy unicorn spotting!